# Serving My Commander

## Taken by My Commander Erotica 4 Stories Bundle

### Mavis Lennon

# Tempted by My Commander

## I was about to let out a sigh of relief when his gaze lingered on me, or more specifically, my breast.

I stood across from the commander as he looked over the plan for the nursing team training. Something about being close to him always made my heart flutter. He was a formidable beast when we fought our enemies and a very tough and hard-to-please boss. Even within the military, he was famous for how strict he was. Maybe I was nervous about that.

The nursing department head had already gone through the plan and gave me a pass. She was satisfied with it and told me to also get a pass from the commander himself.

This wasn't my first time in his office and for sure wasn't the first time I met him in the office alone, but still.... his presence alone could suck the air out of my lungs and also the air out of the room.

Well, to be honest, I was always in his office working closely with him on various projects, but nothing changed despite how many times I was in close proximity to him.

He looked up from the plan to me. His piercing gaze threatened to tear me into shreds. It would be a lot better when he was looking at someone else with that serious look. He was beyond handsome when he was focused. But on the receiving end of that gaze... strangely warmed up my stomach and my pussy clenched.

But I shouldn't think that of him. The commander wouldn't be thinking about that. He was just concerned about the plan and how we could best serve the team.

He said, "The head had approved it?"

"Yes." I swallowed and wanted to hide somewhere away from his gaze. He wasn't mad or anything, but that intensity was also too much to bear.

He nodded. "Good. That let's go forward with it. We can always use more hands on the team."

"Sure." I was about to let out a sigh of relief when his gaze lingered on me, or more specifically, my breast. I was in a shirt, which is the uniform for the unit. Maybe I didn't button it all the way up to my throat, but still... In my defense, it is a hot day in summer.

I asked with my heart racing and almost jumping out of my throat. "Commander, is there... anything else?"

He stood and went to me. My legs were shaking. He was a tall and very muscular man, effectively making me seem tiny. I took half a step back but didn't dare to move more. He demanded all the respect and sometimes fear from everyone. I wasn't the exception.

"You seem to be scared of me."

Yes, but I shouldn't be? I had done nothing wrong, so in theory, I shouldn't be scared. "Why's the question?"

He gave a small smile. "It seems you're shaking by now."

I... He went any closer and his gaze would have melted me. It was one thing when he was across the desk and another when he was this close. "Commander... I..."

"You have nothing to be afraid of."

Except him? Up close, he obviously drained the air from me. He was intimidating enough while he looked great in the leather jacket.

"Commander, I..." I swallowed despite my throat was dry and burning. "I'm not afraid. I'm just..." His gaze still lingered on the opening of my shirt and... fuck...

"What's on your mind for all those stuttering? I don't think I'm that scary." He took another step forward, and I stumbled back. He was too close for me to feel safe. I still remembered how he punished those soldiers and... I knew there was no way he would punish me out of nowhere. But once I've seen that, there was no way I could forget.

I backed onto the wall. He was standing a step away from me. He folded his arms. "Tell me why you're so scared? I understand if you're my enemy, but you know you aren't. Or are you hiding anything from me?"

"No!" I shook my head as quickly and as much as I could. I had been following every guideline. There was nothing I was hiding from him.

His rugged breath landed on me and... my fucking body heated up just from that. I would never admit how much and how long I had been silently staring at him. He was out of my league for sure. I couldn't be the only one either. He was very popular among women on the team; it was just no one dared to approach him. None of us dared to think he would be interested.

He lifted my chin and forced me to meet his eyes. "By any chance, you're hiding your body from me? This is not a command, just a question, and a suggestion."

My mind drew blank. I didn't even know what to do. His voice was rugged and husky. I could feel the lust in his breath. "Commander, I..."

I rested my hand on his chest. He didn't push me away. Maybe he really meant his words and wasn't trying to scout me out. "It is the nursing team member's job to make sure everyone in the army is comfortable."

What was I even rambling about?

He smirked and leaned even closer. His breath was on my lips and his muscular body pressed onto mine. "And will that happen to also include me?"

"I... Why not?" If he didn't back me up to the wall, I would have already dropped onto the floor like a pile of jelly.

His lips crashed into mine, and he squeezed my ass. I closed my eyes while he devoured my lips and my mouth. He could do whatever he wanted to me and I would let him. It was hard to refuse when he was that hot and... that man I had been staring at like a silly brat since the first day I was here.

He pinned my shoulder against the wall with a hand, and he moved to nibble on my throat. His other hand undid the buttons on my shirt, grazing my flesh at times.

He let out a low growl. "You have no idea how tempting you are in this shirt and this skirt."

Both were uniforms, but usually, I would also have my white robe on. But today was a bit too hot, and I wasn't in the facility, so I took it off before heading to his office. That probably was the reason I ended up here between him and the wall.

He lifted my bra and grabbed my boob, rubbing and pinching my nipple. I moaned and my body shook. His rough hand on my sensitive flesh was a bit too much. I reached to undo his belt while he shoved his other hand between my legs. "Fuck, you're so wet. Did coming to my office make you this eager?"

He licked my throat as if I was his prey. That knocked all words out of my brain. He yanked off my panties and rubbed in the pleasure. My clit throbbed with how he thumbed it and how his fingers entered my sex. "Commander, I..."

"You have no idea how much I've been wanting this." He pushed one of my legs to the wall with his. Undid the rest of his belt and fuck it. His cock was a monster. There was no way he could enter me without tearing me apart. He was so large and seemingly so rough for my folds.

Yet all I could do was moan under his fingers and feel how I was soaking up for him. This was to make sure everyone in the army was well taken care of for us to eliminate our enemies. This was part of the job. I refused to admit to myself how much I'd dreamed of this. It felt so wrong to dream that the commander would tear off my clothes and take me like the beast that he was. Yet, this was happening, and I was so ready for him.

He rubbed his tip on my entrance, wetting himself with my juice. "We don't have to go forward with this if you don't want to. Don't be too scared of me to refuse."

Why would I even refuse? Maybe I was soaked enough I could take him in without breaking apart. It was such torture when his cock was a tease and... fuck... I had touched myself while imagining how hard he would take me. "You are so large. Don't kill me with that."

He laughed. "Is this your concern? Don't worry. You're going to like it so much."

His tip stretched me as he entered me. He was so hot and so large that my body tensed and my toes curled. My pussy tried to pull him in, but any faster, and I risked breaking myself. There was a growl from him and he pinched my nipple. "Just relax. I know what I'm doing."

I hummed. Words and any coherent thoughts were so far away from me now. His cock drove my back on the wall and even up the wall. He took over me until he reached the deepest of me with his abs pressed into me. He gasped, so did I. My pussy was trying its best to accommodate him and sucked at his length.

It had been so long since my pussy was filled with something. And commander... This was such a moment for me.

He started moving inside me, his tip devoured my folds and made all those dirty sounds with me. Both with my juice and with how our bodies crashed with each other. "You're so tight. So ready for me."

He picked up speed, ramming harder and harder into me. His size pained me, but it was so great at the same time. I heard that he was a beast in fights and battles and that was the reason how he had risen in ranks rapidly and was now leading our camp. Now, he was taking me like the beast he was.

"You should've let me have you a long time ago." He hissed and his cock throbbed inside me, seemingly even stronger now. He pushed my leg further to the side for him.

My pussy contracted around him so hard that a spark traveled through me and the pleasure hit me hard. I opened my mouth but was too scared that my scream would draw attention. I didn't need others to know how the commander's cock was inside me and I was here with my mind fucked empty.

He leaned in with his shoulder close to my face. I bit him as my body tried to contain a scream from all the pleasure. He chuckled with a husky voice, ramming harder inside me. "Ah, you're such a little brat, huh?"

I yelped softly when he pinched my ass. The pleasure was so strong the surrounding was completely gone. I was here, backed up to a wall, letting him throw me through waves upon waves of pleasure.

He was fucking so hard my feet were off the floor; the gravity making each stroke deeper and harder as our body flushed together and more spark lit my body up into flames.

I couldn't even count the orgasms he threw at me. When he came hard inside me and filled me up with his cum, both of us were panting. His cock was still pulsing inside me. I leaned back on the wall, my body was completely soaked with sweat. If his cock wasn't inside me and if he wasn't holding onto me, I couldn't even remain upright.

He kissed me again and again, now a lot gentler than when he used over me. He was seemingly still hard inside me, while another orgasm had the potential to kill me. "You really should drop by my office more often."

"Sure, commander. I'm yours to want."

He chuckled. His voice was still full of lust. He slowly let go of me and pulled his cock out. I dropped to my knees and took his cock into my mouth. He let out a soft moan as I licked him clean.

This was more than I could hope for. I could never imagine someone like him would take an interest in me. Maybe it was just lust because of my exposed skin and somehow he was horny today, but it was still great regardless. I had no idea how much of a formidable beast he was until now. If this was how he fought, I would really feel sorry for his enemies.

When some strength finally came back to me and when he picked up and gave me my panties, I tried my best to put myself together and look tidy enough to fool everyone. I wasn't supposed to have sex with the commander. Even though he was the rule here and probably no one would dare to report me to him, I still had to be careful and put up my best game.

He hugged me again before I would pick up the document and leave. He felt my pussy and nibbled on my earlobe. "You know no one should know about this."

I nodded. "Otherwise, both of us would be in trouble."

"Smart."

I picked up everything and made sure I looked the same between going into the office and leaving. Walking through the corridor, my sensitive flesh was still complaining about the loss of his touch. His cum was still hot inside me and I had no idea how I could continue the day's work like always.

Back inside the nursing facility, Eve, the head of the department and my direct boss, was near the counter, staring at me. She eyed me up and down as I walked through the entrance. I shivered from that piercing gaze.

She was also a very dominant figure in the camp. If there was someone that dared to talk back to the commander, it would be her.

Eve straightened and gestured for the folder in my hand. "Takes you long enough. What did he say?"

"He... He said it looks good."

She leaned closer and seemingly examined me. "Just that? After spending all the time with you inside his office?"

I had no idea whether that was a genuine question or whether she had found out something and was poking at it. "I mean... he took his time reading over it. I think he must have his own discretion and consideration about the plan."

She mused and glanced at his signature. "Did he ask you anything about the plan?"

I shake my head. It seemed she was holding me around for longer than usual. This wasn't the first time I went to the commander's office, and she had never waited for me at the entrance. These documents weren't emergent anyway.

She must have sniffed out something. Would she kick me out of the camp? That would be a lot easier than trying to get the commander to leave.

What had I done to myself?

Eve gave a curt nod. "I see. Thanks for taking the papers to him then. Get back to work." She walked off toward her office without waiting for my response.

Did this mean I have made it past her eyes? Or did she already know?

# Taunting My Commander

Others wouldn't dare to touch his button, not to mention press it. I was the one that will slam on his button and keep doing that.

It was dead silence in the meeting room. All eyes were on me, and also Kendrick.

Kendrick, the commander of the base camp, glared at me and there were flames in his eyes. "Can you repeat that for me?"

I rolled my eyes. "Sure, in case you weren't listening." I picked up the paper from the table and lifted it to my face. The paper had nothing to do with what I had said, but then I didn't care. He really should learn to listen clearly. "Commander, your plan is one of the silliest ones I've heard in a while. Our supply chain isn't going to catch up that soon and we should wait for that before you plan to lead the team in an almost suicide mission."

He growled, "That's not a suicide mission. It is not any more impossible or dangerous than what we have been doing before. Supply chain, supply chain. You keep spilling that nonsense. We have to carry out the plan so that the supply can keep coming in. How about you use — You should look into things happening beside us instead of just thinking with you — with those basics."

I snorted a laugh, mostly from how he was trying to stop himself with those insults. I was the one who never cared. Everyone knew I was mean in that way, so that was expected. He was the one who loved to remain pristine for everyone.

The few leaders among us were staring at one another. It was pretty rare for me and the commander to be arguing in the open, though that had happened before. Why did they all look surprised?

I said, "Trying so hard to be polite? Aren't you already swearing under your breath? Anyway, our supply is coming in fine. Those disgusting things wouldn't get them that easily. We have an escort team to help them and it has been doing fine. You can want to be proactive, but it makes no sense when the medical supplies are running low. It's more risk than the team can take. How about you also look through the basics?"

He glared at me, his whole body tensed. I was the only one in the camp who dared to keep challenging him. If it was someone else they would have given up already. That were some gazes that promised to choke you alive.

There was a warmth inside me and pussy contracted. Maybe I was that bad at separating his intense gaze at work from the one I would get when he had me naked on his desk. Would he think of that?

We were all sitting around the round meeting room table, so there was no way to tell without getting to see his cock. It would surely be interesting to check on that.

His gaze burned me hot, and he probably was fucking me in his mind, not just with his words.

He said, "Doc, what smart thing do you have instead?"

"Smart for you to say that. Obviously, I have a better plan. It's on the third page of the meeting agenda. Just read it."

I loved watching him fuming. It wasn't even hard to rile him up. Others wouldn't dare to touch his button, not to mention press it. I was the one that will slam on his button and keep doing that.

He grabbed the agenda and flipped it, all the same time with his menacing gaze on me. If we were sitting closer, maybe he would've grabbed me and growled in my face. Or maybe not. He knew how to keep acting appropriately for a meeting.

Others also flipped over to that page. They probably had already read it. They were a very dependable crew. I had confidence in them. Commander probably also had read it and simply needed a refresher.

I said, "Mostly, I'm just suggesting that we postpone your suggestion to after the supply is here. We should send more out to help the transporting team, but then it isn't smart to hunt for those creatures' lair right now. Those things don't sleep and their senses are still a mystery. Your time would be better spent training the new ones here."

Kendrick was quiet as he looked through my plan. I loved his serious face, that was the best after his face that was so pissed off by me. To be honest, while I'd argued with him before, seldom would he get this angry.

It probably had to do with how I called him a meaty head earlier in front of the crew. He obviously didn't enjoy that. This man wouldn't take a joke.

He eventually said, "We should still make the transporting team's path smoother by removing some obstacles."

Fuck, that gaze was here again, and the intensity was making me wet. I knew he probably wasn't trying to nudge me that way, but it had been a while since we last met up. Maybe my body was craving him a bit too much. That was silly.

I said, "What obstacles?"

"Other armies. Also places those creatures can hide in and ambush us."

"Are you suggesting a patrol to check those all out?"

"Yes, you finally have some senses?" He snickered. He probably was happy that we were finally reaching some kind of consensus. We weren't in his office now, otherwise, I would have come up with something just to get him mad and for me to get a good view.

I said, "I'm always the sensible one here. Meaty head. My main point is to try not to have any injuries, so we don't load the infirmary too hard. Otherwise, you can do whatever plan you want. You're the one in charge, after all."

He huffed, seeming still mad at being called names by me. The crew was tense, and they were making sure they didn't become the next on the chopping board. He asked, "So, you all. We'll change over the mission to a patrolling one and the main assault will be pushed to after the supply is ready. Any concerns?"

With that gaze and that dominating tone, I doubted he would receive any questions. He would never be mean to those, not like to me. He was the best leader I've met in a while and he had all my respect despite me keeping pissing him off.

The crew shook their heads. Kendrick nodded. "Good, then that's nailed down now. From each of your team, get me five to join this mission while keeping others still on the daily patrol. If you have no questions, the meeting will end here."

I would have said that he should also ask for my questions instead of not even looking at me. But I had nothing to add, and I didn't plan on wasting everyone's time when I would end up simply messing with Kendrick.

The crew packed their things, but then they remained in their seats. Kendrick was still in his seat while, usually, he was the one leaving first and everyone would follow him. He was the commander here.

Kendrick gestured for them to leave, so they stood and left, closing the door behind them.

I lifted a brow at him after we were the only ones left in the room. His mouth opened and before he told me to also leave, I asked, "Commander, aren't you the first to leave and that'll suit your title more?"

He huffed. "You have to keep messing with me? I don't care about my title more than my team."

"You know I mean well. Just want to keep the casualty low. You know I care about them no less than you."

He nodded, but he remained in his chair with his legs under the table.

I asked, "Why aren't you leaving then? I thought you have stuff to do back in your office."

There was a flash in his eyes, the one with intensity and temptingly dark. "What are you suggesting? I'll leave when I want to."

"Just that? Leaving? You meaty head."

He growled, "You have to keep doing this?" He looked around. We were the only ones in the room. He gestured for me to go to him. I smirked and shook my head.

He said, "Scared of me?"

I remembered that gaze on me. Now it was lingering, kind of there, but not as strong. "What are you planning?"

"Come over and you'll know."

I was curious. I headed over to him. The fire was still in my stomach. Since I first had a go with him, when there were only the two of us in a room, there was always a spark of something between us that I couldn't point a finger at.

When I was a few steps away from him, he spun from his seat, grabbed me into his arms, and pressed his lips onto mine.

His scent and his strong lips made my body weak. I held onto him and let his tongue devour me. His hardness pressed against me, his erection was palpable and it was now obvious why he didn't leave with the crew.

I loved how he held me close. His muscular body was amazing. His chest pressed against my boobs, and his warmth was comforting.

I rubbed my pussy against his hard cock. Our clothes were annoyingly existing on our bodies. I gasped and pulled away from him before he would set me on fire. "Ah, naughty, huh?"

He hissed. "You are prompting this. You should've just kept your mouth shut."

I snorted a laugh. "Seriously? You just want my mouth open when you want to fuck that? Not happening. I have the team's best interest in mind, not yours."

"Even then, you don't have to call me names." He took my hand and rested it on his erection, which I would be doing in a few seconds. He was so large and so promising. "You are asking for this."

"For what?" I put up an innocent face. "I don't under-stand what you're talking about."

"Calling me a meaty head?"

I rubbed his cock, and he twitched under my hand. "Do you not have something meaty for me?"

"You are insufferable." He groaned and shook his head. I loved it when he was so annoyed with me, but he had to try to be a decent man and not beat up a woman like me.

I shrugged. "So we don't have a problem now?"

He gestured to the door. "Lock it. You need to be put back in your place."

The flame in my stomach came back stronger. Was he saying what I think he was saying? "My place? I'm very comfortable with my place on the team. What do you mean?"

He let out a husky breath with those beat-like gazes. Maybe he was already fucking me in his mind. I was pretty certain about it. "Are you going to lock the door or not?"

I shrugged. "You always think you can make me — Hey!"

He rubbed my pussy, and he smirked. "I can feel it. Now, before you walk away soaked wet, just lock the door."

He had me wrapped between his fingers, huh?

I headed over to the door. "Maybe you should consider doing that yourself. Or your hard cock making it hard to walk?"

He growled, "No."

Except I probably nailed it. It probably wouldn't be comfortable to walk around with a hard cock. His meaty head rubbing against the fabric would be no fun.

I locked the door. There were no windows here, so it was only the two of us here, alone. "Now what?"

He was leaning on the table, staring at me.

I said, "What? Undressing me in your mind already?"

He huffed and gestured for me to get closer. When I did, he said, "Kneel, you should learn to. Fuck — "

"Swearing doesn't look good on you." I laughed when he seemingly was shocked I had already taken his cock out in my hands.

"Dammit. You know how to surprise." He let out a soft moan as I stroked his length. He was so hard and so large that I can't even hold him with a hand.

"You'd never expect me to do what you want? You know I always call out your crap and I don't care whether there are others around."

He grabbed my head and shoved his cock into my mouth. He probably had been thinking about that the moment I said his plan wasn't going to work. Well, given I was pretty rude with the words I used, he should understand that was because I respected him and held him to a high standard.

I opened my mouth wider to take in his cock. He was large, and it was hard to accommodate him. He thrust deep into my throat, his cock pulsing inside me. He chuckled. "Look at you. This is where you should be, sucking my cock."

Except he was the one grabbing my head to make sure he could get into my throat. One would have thought it only counted when I did it myself. But then his cock made it hard to utter a word, and I hated it.

He moved inside me, forcefully taking my every breath. I held the base of his cock, making him slow his strokes. He would choke me alive and it wouldn't look good outside.

He hissed. "Come on. What are you scared of?"

I wanted so much to smack him in the head with my words, but his cock kept moving and it was getting hard to even think. There were only moaning noises from me and the sound of him fucking my mouth.

He grabbed tighter on my hair, but he didn't pull on me. Otherwise, he probably knew I wouldn't play along. He said, "You have no idea how much I've been wanting to fuck my cock into your mouth and shut you up. You have this. Fucking. Annoying. Mouth."

Dammit, he hammered in those hard strokes when he uttered those words. Of course, he hated my words. I was here to check on him when I was second in command shall anything happen to him, which I would never hope to happen.

I licked him as he let out his anger at me. I kind of liked it. Whenever he took me with force and with those tempting intensity, I was all for it.

He growled, "Look at me, doc."

I did. He gasped. I liked how he fucked my mouth in his uniform. I had a thing for that. When he stripped me naked on his desk, his cock hammering in pleasure, he looked amazing in those uniforms.

He hissed, "Have you learned to not be a bitch and just listen to me?"

If he intended for me to answer, he needed to get his cock away from me, but I doubted he would.

He kept hammering into me and I had to try my best to not puke. His cock kept irritating my throat, but lit a fire in my stomach.

"Doc, you always love to provoke me." He pulled out of me when his cock was throbbing and he was getting close.

I smirked. Now, I could finally talk back to my annoying commander. "Well, commander, that's the easiest thing I've ever done. You've always wanted to fuck me. Even when we were in a strategic meeting, when everyone should focus on developing a good combat plan? And all you can think about is to fuck my mouth."

He growled, "Must you? You know that I'm serious about work."

"But your erection is so hard that you can't even stand to leave. Who are you fooling? Yourself? Commander — !" Before I could end my sentence, he grabbed me and put me on the table with his monstrous strength.

"Can you just shut the fuck up?" He grabbed my boob and squeezed just hard enough to make my pussy clench.

"I thought you like my mouth. What are you going to do with me, commander?"

He reached under my dress and yanked off my panties with such a smooth motion that it seemed like he had done that more times than he could count.

He rubbed my pussy and clenched my clit. I shivered, and a moan escaped me. He smirked. "Look at you, doc. You're so wet. Maybe you just want to piss me off and get wet on the way."

"You're thinking too highly of yourself. Mm..."

He teased my entrance with his fully ready cock. "Tell me that again?"

"You think you can shut me up with your cock? Silly you. No way — !" I yelped when he probed my cunt with the tip of his cock, but pulled out before my cunt could pull him deep inside me.

"Tell me again how you don't want me?" He sneered with that annoyingly handsome face. "Doc, be honest with yourself. You're just a horny woman. Is your pussy aching after merely a while of not having me?"

I squirmed on the table. I hated how he enjoyed teasing me. He was making the lust inside me hard to bear. "I'm not. You're the horny one who wants to shove your cock somewhere. Admit it, you want my pussy."

He glared at me with that gaze, the gaze that implied that he was probably already fucking me in his mind. He rubbed his length over my pussy, such a tease while leaving me empty.

"Commander..."

"You know what to do."

My cunt contracted and craved for some of him, no, all of him. "You're such a tease."

He chuckled. By now, he knew my body well. And it didn't help when my juice was making his cock shiny and look tasty. "Doc, it seems it is my turn to cure how much of a bad woman you are."

"Oh yeah? What does that entail?"

"A dose of my cock? How does it sound? Want it?"

"If it's good, I'll want it."

He growled and entered me, stretching me for himself.

"Yes, commander."

When he leaned over and hammered his cock inside me, he took off the rest of my clothes and played with my boobs. "Look at you, such a little slut. If you want me to fuck you hard, you can just ask. There's no need to cause a scene in the meeting."

"You are the one thinking about shoving your cock inside me during the meeting."

"As if you aren't? Don't lie. When you argue with me, you know what's going to happen."

Let his cock dominate all my senses? I moaned when he hammered those hard strokes into the deepest of me. He had his way of varying his strokes' length and strength, all in the attempt to screw me over.

Every time when I needed him to ram deep inside me, he teased me with those light strokes. When I wanted to catch a breath, he hammered into the deepest of me. He was always this annoying.

I reached to hug him when he took my wrists and pinned my hands over my head on the table. It made my boobs juggle and looked even larger for him, which he probably enjoyed with how his cock twitched inside me. "Commander..."

"You should know your place. You're much better off here than running your mouth around here."

"Here? Being my commander's fuck toy?"

"Dammit." His cock throbbed, and he slowed his strokes.

"No! Don't stop." I was getting that close to an orgasm, but he fucking stopped. How annoying. My pussy clenching tight onto him, wanting him deeper.

He gasped. He was holding out before he would come inside me. I understood that, but I was hanging on the edge and he left me empty. He should at least stay inside for my pussy to suck him.

He said, "Why the hurry? Admit it, you want to get cocks in your pussy."

"Commander... you know I want you. Also, admit it, my pussy is squeezing you so hard that you can hold another second inside me. It's a shame if I make you come before you get me screaming — Oh! Yes! More!"

He shoved his cock inside me, pounding my pussy even harder. "Look at you, grabbing me so tight."

Those strokes caused the fireworks inside me. I screamed when the orgasm hit me hard. He covered my mouth at once, but the meeting room was absolutely soundproof to the outside.

He smirked. Maybe he just wanted to quiet me, which made the pleasure even stronger when the only exit for it was to torment my pussy and stay inside my body.

I moaned and my toes arched when he picked up speed and rubbed my clit. He knew how to play with my body. His cock grew harder now, taking me with his force. He lifted one of my legs, resting it on his shoulder when he fucked me even harder. He felt larger and being spread even wider stirred a wave of shame inside me.

My commander was having his way with my pussy and all I could do was lay here and let him devour me. In the war zone, he made everyone else his prey, and now, I was his captured little prey. Worse, a prey that was lured to him by his cock and now having what I wanted destroying me.

"Commander... Oh! Fuck! I... Yes...!" I had no idea what I was uttering by now. Those probably weren't even words. He smirked as he continued throwing me up the highs, making each wave of pleasure stronger than the last one.

I wouldn't last long under him. His cock would make me his little slut and I fucking loved how rough he was with me. "Commander..."

His cock twitched. "Doc, you need your commander to heal you and remind you little slut who you actually are, right?"

Words escaped me again when another storm of pleasure swept me off my feet. I was moaning and squirming now. Another orgasm would break me beyond repair.

"Doc, it's your turn for an injection." His cock twitched, and he pinned himself deep inside me. His cock erupted inside me, giving me all his hot cum.

I moaned and squirmed. He was coming so hard and he filled me at once. He filled me until I was overflowing and until it was dripping out of me despite his cock inside me. I gasped. "It seems you've been wanting to empty your sac."

He chuckled. "Saving it to cure how horny you are." He pulled out and the mixture of his cum and my juice was dripping out of me as my pussy contracted, crying for the loss of his hardness.

I remained on the floor, staring blankly at the ceiling. He always did all the dirty things to me, and I had no way of resisting him. Not complaining, though, my body also wanted him.

He rubbed my pussy and slapped it. I shivered and my pussy contracted, dripping more of his cum. I would smack his shoulder if I had the strength to get up.

"Doc, when you need another cure, feel free to ask." He smirked, the way he was when his enemies tripped and failed.

"You'll have to get me off the table first. I hate you…"

"Really? Ask your pussy then. Does it hate me?"

I really would smack him if I could.

He gave me a hand and helped me sit on the table instead of laying. He held me to his side while I gasped and tried to regain my energy. Who could've guessed it was so tiring even when I was laying down to get fucked?

But being the monster he was, he wasn't even panting anymore.

I rubbed his abs despite his clothes were still there. "You aren't tired? You're so strong."

"Well, I have to take care of everyone. Can't afford to not be strong."

Ah, my very respected and dependable commander. He could do whatever he wanted to me and I would like it.

But if his goal was to get me to shut up in meetings, he was failing. It was even more tempting to rile him up than before.

# Taking Care of My Commander

We may have minutes, if not seconds, before we would lose him. I couldn't let that happen.

"Hurry up!" I shouted as the stretchers and the wounded soldiers were sent back to the facility after another mission. My heart was pumping at full speed as I ran down to the ground floor of the facility. As the head of the medical team, I had to be there with everyone.

Most of the nurses were already there mending soldiers and triaging them. I hated how we needed to triage them and couldn't treat everyone all at once..

A stretcher was pushed to me. One of the soldier's legs was blown off by an explosive. Before that nurse could open her mouth, I pointed to the corridor behind me. "OR 3, now."

"Tell us where to go!" There was a growl from a soldier. I spun around.

Helen was standing there staring at a stretcher, not making a voice.

What the fuck was she doing?

I dashed over there, pushing two other workers to the side. My blood almost froze when I saw what Helen saw.

The commander was on a barely put-together stretcher. His eyes were closed and there was a large wound on his stomach. The fabric of his clothes and the oozing blood meshed together. On his face were fragments of debris and more blood.

Another crew with a decent stretcher arrived. I calmed myself. We may have minutes, if not seconds, before we would lose him. I couldn't let that happen. "Helen! Get him over to the stretcher and into operation."

"I..." She stumbled and her hands were shaking.

This was absolutely useless.

I shoved her to the side and shouted for another soldier to take her place. We moved the commander and rushed him into the operation room.

It ended up to be a busy and very long day of running around different operation rooms and mending a lot of wounds. Even when I was out of the field for now, it seemed the smell of blood was still lingering in my nose. I let out a heavy sigh and sipped on my coffee in my office, rubbing my temple.

I would have stayed there if my coworkers didn't kick me out of there. They thought that just because I hadn't eaten breakfast and lunch meant I couldn't keep going with the evening shift. How silly.

I checked my phone, no messages and no missed calls, which was good news for sure. For the nursing team, no news was the best thing.

There was a knot in my stomach, and I almost threw up. I shivered and winced. But as I closed my eyes, the commander covered in his own blood flashed into my mind.

I gasped and snapped my eyes open. He was fine. I knew that. I was the one wheeling him into the resting room after the operation. I was the one connecting the detectors on him and I had made sure he was breathing and his heart was beating before I left to treat others.

Commander... Who would have guessed?

I hated this, but there was nowhere to go when there were all those... disgusting creatures roaming cities and places that I once called home.

Maybe I should go and check on him. I hoped he would wake up soon, but I wasn't hopeful. And maybe he would need all the time to take a rest.

I still went out of my office and to the floor of those rooms. At the door, Helen was there, pacing around the door. I scowled. She wasn't part of this shift. Why was she here?

"Helen." How she stumbled and froze earlier today came back into my mind. Something was off here.

She shuddered as she saw me, and she hurried to step back. "Head, good evening."

I tilted my head to the side. "What are you doing here?"

She looked to the side. "Nothing. And I'm sorry for what happened this morning. I..."

"That's also what I wanted to talk to you about. You aren't that way in any other day." I narrowed my eyes at her. "The commander would have died."

"I know..." she sobbed. "I really am sorry. I don't even know what I was doing there. Please tell me he's fine?"

It seemed she really cared about him. And... other than that one time I caught her seemingly spending more time than needed in his office, there were more times she seemingly had sneaked out of her shift to who knew where. I trusted her to take over a lot of my work, which included taking document to the commander. Apparently, something interesting had happened.

I nodded. "He's in recovery now. We have to put him into a comma to stabilize him. All things considered, he's fine."

She let out a heavy sigh of relief. "That's good to know, thank you."

"Why are you so caring for him?"

She snapped her head up and stared at me. "No! I... I mean, everyone worries about him, right? He's the commander, after all."

That was still suspicious. But she likely wouldn't tell me if I didn't have solid evidence in my hand. "You've had quite a day already. Just take a rest."

"Sure." She nodded and hurried away.

Still suspicious, but I didn't have the time to take care of that for now.

Inside the corridor, it was mostly quiet by now. All the injured soldiers were bandaged and resting. Those that... we had lost... were already sent away. I walked by the corridor and gave the patrolling nurse a nod before I headed to the guarded area where the commander was taking a rest.

He was in the room deep inside the corridor. I stopped by the window. He was still in bed with his eyes closed. There was a surge of pain in my chest as I stared at his almost lifeless form. That wasn't the man I had known.

Maybe I shouldn't have grown close to him. It would make the surgery earlier a lot easier. I almost couldn't do it and I probably was too close to him to perform it to his good, but I was the only that could at that moment, and no one should know the things between him and I.

Given, there was no string between us, it still... affected me more than anything else.

I went into the room and take a seat by his side. I didn't think I can sleep through the night. Maybe I should stay here and watch him instead.

He stirred and opened his eyes.

What? He wasn't supposed to wake up now. We were guessing not before the next morning.

He gave me a small smile. "Eve..."

I held his hand at once, making sure I wouldn't disturb the tubes on him. "Hey. Guess it's good that I'm here? Wasn't expecting you to wake up this soon."

"Really?" He coughed, and I was going to call for support when he managed to stop. "Sorry, I think I'm a lot better now. Thank you."

I stroked his cheek. "It's my job to keep you alive."

He mused and let out a tensed breath. "I should be more careful."

I shook my head. "You're still alive. That's enough for me."

He rubbed my knuckles. "I guess I'll spare the evaluation with my fellow."

I let out a soft chuckle. "I guess so. For me in the nursing unit, your survival is the most important thing and the only thing I'm concerned about."

He closed his eyes and checked the monitor for his vital signs at once. Nothing was out of place. Maybe he was just tired. He said with a voice almost a whisper, "You'll be here with me, right?"

"Of course." I wouldn't leave him even if the other staff dragged me.

He hummed. A silence lingered between us. It was a silence I could get comfortable in.

"Hey." I nudged him. Seeing how Helen froze staring at him when he was wounded had piped too much of my curiosity.

"Yes?"

"Helen."

He visibly tensed and his blood pressure, as seen on the monitor, raise. "What?"

It would take a blind to not know something was happening. "Who. The nurse I've been sending your way with the documents."

He cleared his throat. "I know who Helen is. I mean, why are you mentioning her?"

"When they brought you back from the fields and you were badly injured. She should be the one assigning you to a team and get your treated, but she froze staring at you. Very unusual for her. She may not be around as long as both of us did, but she for sure was experienced enough."

He scowled. "Are you implying something?"

I liked him. With him, I would never need to spell things out. "Both of us are smart enough, right?"

"I have no idea what you are driving towards."

It seemed he would need a bit more hints. Or maybe he was trying to hide things from me. Interesting. "Recently, it has taken her longer and longer with the documents that would require your eyes on them. Is there anything wrong with the papers?"

"I just prefer to give those a closer look and careful eyes."

"Just that? You know me. I'm not someone that'll let you off the hook easily."

His frown deepened. He should know nothing could pass me with me knowing. He said, "I have no idea what you're talking about." Except the vital sign trackers were more like a lie-detector now. Though I didn't need those to spot that. We had known each other for too long to need the help of a device.

"Helen's my subordinate."

"So? I still don't see — Hey!" He shivered when I rest my hand on his cock. He twitched as I stroked him over his trousers. "What does this even mean? You aren't implying I've laid my hands on her, right?"

"What is so wrong about that? You and I..."

He winced. "Nothing can slide past you, right? She told you?"

I pecked a kiss on his cheek. Under a situation with this high tension, I could understand that. He and I also... heated up because of that. A good way to blow off some steam and we had made sure for it to have no string attached. "Of course she won't. I've danced around the topic. She is nervous about it for sure."

"You aren't going to punish her, right?"

Something about him... I guess I really liked him. His cock was now harder under my hand. If needed, it wouldn't take long for him to snap and tell me everything. This was also something special between us. "Of course not. It's fair game, right? I know I haven't had the time to see you a lot. But apparently, you've found a solution to that."

"Eve." He reached a hand up to my face. I leaned down for him to stroke me before he would pull on the tubes on his hand. He said, "I don't know. I was just... feeling the urge that day and since... You really won't punish her, right?"

"Between you and me, you know who's the rules here. She's my subordinate."

He swallowed. "But it really wasn't her fault for what had happened — "

"That had happened for more time than you can count. I mean, I would appreciate it if you would've dropped me a word."

"Well..." He shuddered as my hand moved from his cock to his abs. The wound was on one side, leaving enough room on the other for me to stroke him.

"Be honest with me?"

"I don't owe you anything. We've made it clear that there's no string attached between us." He almost growled and I shivered from that glare on me. For his recovering body, that must be hard. Maybe I had overstepped.

"Sorry..." I took my hand back to myself. "I don't mean to overstep. Are you in pain now?"

He sighed. "I understand, though. If I've caught wind that you had something with another man, I guess I would also have asked."

I leaned into his ear. "I haven't had time with you for a while, and you're hungry putting your claws on my assistant."

"You're jealous."

"I'm not," I lied, and he smirked, seemingly already saw through me.

Maybe I was a bit jealous. I knew how great he was with the action. I could never have enough of him. Knowing he had touched another woman didn't sit that well with me. But like what we had agreed on, he and

I were... just comrades in the war zone. Not dating and for sure wasn't in a committed relationship.

Helen was younger than me and also a very attractive woman. I wasn't at all surprised about that. Knowing Kendrick, my commander, he would take whatever he wanted.

I swallowed. "Maybe a bit. You know I miss you. It's just... with the newest research, I seldom have the time to step outside of the lab and the facility."

He stroked my cheek. "I also miss you."

I rested my forehead on his. "When you get better, I'll hold that against you."

His eyes darkened. "That may be quite a wait."

"All the more motivation for me to get you back into one piece." My pussy clenched as I uttered those words. I had always wanted him. Now that I couldn't, I wanted him even more. I was such a slut.

He smirked. "I like you for that." He lifted his other hand, which was in a better condition than the one closer to me. "So I have your word, right? When I've recovered, you'll spend more time with me."

"You just want to fuck me."

My cheeks were burning. That was an exception. I didn't even know what I was doing that day, and he would never stop mentioning that every time he wanted to tease me and shame me. I pinched his shoulder. "Stop it. You know I don't mean that."

"You don't mean what? I don't think there's a way to read that in another way. You grabbed my belt and pushed me to the wall."

I had no interest in arguing that with him. I just want him to still be here, still breathing and still living. "Commander... Stop teasing me?"

He rested his hand on my head and stroked me. I liked how gentle he could be. He nodded, despite there seemed to still be pain on his face. "Sure. Somehow, I like that coming from you. You remember the time when you argued with me in the meeting? When everyone is going commander with me, you shouted my first name and made me look like a kid."

"Just stop it already."

"Before you know it, I'll fuck you so hard you can't even get off the desk."

"Oh yeah? And it seems if I want to revenge, I'll only have now. You've already proved to be a stronger man than all the medicals had expected."

He blinked. "What are you going to do with me, Doc?"

I looked behind my back through the window at the corridor. No one was there, just like I expected, and there probably wouldn't be anyone walking past until the next morning. But I still lowered the blind and locked the door.

He chuckled. "Apparently, you're planning to play naughty and dirty.'

I lifted his blanket and felt his cock. He was already hard and touching him lit a fire in my stomach. "If you aren't injured, I would have ridden you. You're so hard."

"Well, I'd say I'm so ready for you. But apparently," he lifted his hand with the tubes, "apparently, I have to stay here and can't actually fuck you. I'm so hard it hurts."

Fuck him. I really wanted him. I stroked his length. His cock twitched and grew harder and thicker. "After you've recovered... you have to do what you've said."

I licked his tip, liking how he tasted. I could see how he would take me in my mind and I wanted him so much.

He moaned. "Eve..." When I took in his length, he grabbed my hair fucking my mouth with his monster-like cock. He could choke me with his cock, but I liked it. If it would help take his attention away from his pain and the injury, it would be good enough for me.

I knew him. He probably hated every minute he was stuck on the bed.

"Commander, morning." I gave him a smile.

He sat up from the bed on his own. There were no more tubes on him and no more constant monitoring was needed. "Morning. Good to see you. Are you here to release me from this jail?"

"The bed? I bet your soldiers would love another second on it."

He licked his lips. "If you're going to be on it, then I won't mind staying here for a moment longer."

My heart skipped a beat. While I was already anticipating it and I was already wet when I came into his room, I wasn't expecting him to suggest this. We had never fucked on a bed. Most of the time, we had it in his office, or my lab. It would be a disaster for me to be in his room when he slept with other soldiers. "Are you sure you're ready for it?"

"For you? I'm always ready."

I tapped my pen on the clipboard and bit my lower lip. "I'll take the invitation. But then we have to tackle the important thing first." I pointed the pen at him. "We've checked everything with you and did all the examinations. So you can leave after lunch. I bet you can't wait."

He lifted my chin and guided me onto the bed. "There is something else I can't wait for."

"Commander, I..."

He pulled me over his body, his hardness pressed against my already soaked pussy. "You've promised to ride me."

"Fine." I would rather he bend me over his desk, grab the back of my neck and fuck me until I faint. But whatever ways I could have his cock, I would be happy enough.

While I took his cock, he yanked off my panties and cupped my pussy, rubbing my clit. "Commander..."

"You like this, huh? Now get started and ride my cock."

I shivered from that tone, the tone he used to instruct his soldiers. Somehow, that always turned me on. I moved to hover over him, his tip already grazing my entrance.

He smacked my ass. "I said ride me already."

I moaned and took his cock inside me. He stretched me and he was so hot and so tasty. I had no idea how much my body craved him until now. I needed his touch on me and his cock inside me.

He grabbed my boobs and thrust up at my pussy. I stumbled and crashed onto him, his cock rammed into the deepest of me. "Eve, good job. Now rock your ass like the good little slut you are."

I bit the inside of my mouth and started taking him in and out of me, letting him take over my body.

He had a cold gaze on me, the way that would turn me on so much and could make me come so hard. "Good, doc. I like how your cunt is squeezing on me. Work harder for your own pleasure."

"Yes... commander." The pleasure built inside me, slowly wrapping its fingers around me, fanning the fire in my stomach.

"Harder. If you don't want to be here, just get off me. Let me have someone that actually wants this."

Dammit! He really could talk... I picked up speed, taking him harder and deeper into me. He thrust up at times, his cock entered me so much deeper than I could manage.

"Commander, I..."

"Don't come until I let you."

Fuck him! I gritted my teeth when he grabbed my ass and guided how I moved and how I fucked myself over with his cock. The fire was threatening to burn me alive and holding the pleasure was almost impossible. "Please? I can't!"

"I said wait for my approval," his low growl grabbed onto me, forcing me to take in all the torturous strokes. His cock twitched inside me and grew hotter.

I couldn't hold on any longer with that hard and hot cock inside me. His gaze did the job for me. He stared at me as if I was the slut that was begging for him, inviting him to devour my body until I was a messy pile for him.

"Show me what you've got, slut."

I screamed when he came inside me. He grabbed my ass and forced me to take in all of his hot cum. Not that I would ever refuse anyway. The orgasm I had been holding back erupted inside me. The waves crashed onto me until my whole body tensed, trying to not drown and die from the high.

He held onto my waist. Otherwise, I would have collapsed. His cock was still pulsing. I was so full of him down there. He said, "Good work. I guess it's not that bad an idea to let you ride my cock. You always have the tightest and dirtiest pussy."

The coldness in his eyes slowly faded, giving me the gaze that was how we usually chatted with. He hugged me and kissed my temple, trailing his way to my throat.

Once he found out how he could turn me on with a cold glare and shouting commands at me, he would never let me off the hook. It was great when we had sex together, but caused trouble once when we argued in a meeting with others in the room. Probably no one had found out how soaked I was when he and I were shouting at each other.

"Commander... you feel better now? Fully recovered?" I snuggled to his chest and ran my fingers over the scar on his stomach. The scar would stay there for another while, otherwise, he was golden.

"Hm... I think I'm good enough. But I still think some check-ups at times will help. You can arrange that, right? Doc. Inside my office, with your legs spread and ass lifted."

Sounded like I was the one getting checked instead. Anyway, of course, I could check on him all day and make sure he could give me those sweet fucks. "Let me know when you'll need those."

My commander would be back at his full capacity in no time. Which involved taking me like the beast he was and making sure I would obey his every command.

# Confronting My Commander

## He had no idea who was knocking. Good.

Author's note: This takes another turn from Taking Care of My Commander, which you have just read. What if Eve has nothing with Kendrick before the incident in the hospital?
The following picks up from Kendrick's successful operation. If you have skipped it, you may want to get back to the start for full context.

I went into the commander's office. Supposedly, he had already recovered, and I had given him a few days of rest. I still couldn't shake how Helen stood there and stared at him when he was badly injured and unconscious. Helen wasn't that. She was my very dependable assistant, and she had never frozen in front of anyone. There had to be something between Helen and the commander.

It is already late in the day now, but there's still light from this office despite the lowered blinds. No one dared to disturb him and no one would want to stand before that gaze. He had that intensity that would threaten to burn everything in front of him.

But I was pretty certain he and Helen had something going on. And even before I knew that, I've never backed down from him.

I knocked, and there were footsteps coming to the door. Apparently, he was planning to kick me out instead of calling for me to go inside. He had no idea who was knocking. Good.

He yanked the door open and was about to snap at me. But he halted when he met my eyes. He scowled and cleared his throat. "What's the issue?" He walked to the side to let me into his office. "You haven't told me you're coming."

I shrugged. My heart was racing from his gaze. He had a presence that was intimidating enough. I had been working with him in the camp for a long time and we had been through a lot of battles together, yet sometimes, he still had that and it still always worked on me. But I simply refused to back off at times. "Who do you think you are? I have to book a time with you?"

His hand moved. Apparently, he wanted to slap me, but he stopped himself. "What's the deal? You seem pissed."

I headed into the room, and half sat on his desk. He let out a low growl. I knew it would taunt him. One thing both of us shared was how we both had an ego a bit too strong. "Helen."

He tensed, and his eyes widened for a split second before he calmed himself. He was the man leading the team, after all, so I would give him that. He said, "I don't understand."

"How's your wound now? Healed up?"

He felt his stomach where the scar was. I was the one doing the stitches. His gaze seemingly softened. "You're here to check me up? But then it doesn't feel that way."

I smirked. He wasn't that dumb after all. "I did the stitches, so I don't have to check. I know it is perfect." I didn't, but he wouldn't know anyway.

"Then what are you here for?"

"I said, Helen."

"I also said I don't know what you mean."

I gestured for him to come closer. He hated it. Anyone tried to make him do things and he would be pissed, especially if those were useless and stupid stuff, like how I waved my finger at him. He folded his arms and snorted, not moving a step. "Just spill it."

"That day when you're injured, she froze on the spot and stared at you like a dummy. I had to push her to the side to get you on a stretcher so that you didn't end up dead."

He lifted an eyebrow. "Cut to the chase. Are you here wanting me to thank you or what?"

"Thank me? Stop degrading me. Trying my best to save everyone is my job."

He frowned again. Either he was trying to skirt what happened between him and Helen, or he thought I knew nothing.

I said, "Helen froze at the spot and she had never done that before."

His face gave away nothing.

I repeated, "She froze there and couldn't move a step. What's the reason? That day, there were injured ones who had it much worse than you, but she didn't even flinch."

"Are you implying something?" He was almost growling. I bit the inside of my mouth to stop myself from shivering.

I had to try so hard to keep my voice stable. He was intimidating enough. He was a large man and demanded respect for him just by existing. I said, "You've touched her."

"No."

"Too fast, not convincing at all."

He took in a breath. "Don't make things up. Maybe she's just scared. Seldom do I get injured."

I laughed. "Seriously? She's trained to conduct emergency service. You think she's going to be scared because of your injury? Are you seriously looking down on her and also me? I'm the one training her."

He clenched a fist, but remained silent.

I continued, "And, when I tell her to bring you documents, it seems to always take her a lot longer than it is reasonable. I wonder what happened."

"Go ask her."

"Is she going to tell me what you've done to her?"

"Stop accusing me with your imagination."

I liked how he seemed so confident. I got off the desk and headed to him. "You know I'm not lying. How can you do that to her?"

He hissed and stared down at me with his height. Annoyingly, he was a head taller than me. And even more annoyingly, he was a lot larger and more muscular than me. Even though it was normal when he was a man and I was a woman, it was still annoying. He leaned closer and snarled. "I've done nothing."

"How long should we play this game? I understand if you have some kind of need."

He glared at me but didn't drop a word. It seemed he finally realized that I knew what had happened.

I gave his shoulder a squeeze. Sometimes I didn't know what he thought of me. In meetings, I was the only one that would push back against him. I was sure he hated me for that. But then we also worked closely on different strategies and battles. He was a trusted comrade, but he could still hate me.

"Commander, admit it. Helen is an attractive woman, right?"

His lips pressed into a thin line, and his glare could kill. If I was just a random soldier, maybe he was considering killing me off and hiding my body, as well as his secret somewhere no one would ever find out. "I have nothing to admit."

"It's wrong to fuck around."

"I said I've never done what you're accusing me of."

"You think I'm blind? I can see how she always comes back from your office. Commander, if I'm looking to cause you trouble, we won't even be here talking."

He let out a heavy, but still calculating breath. "What do you stand to gain? They aren't getting rid of me any-time soon."

"I'm just suggesting for you to keep your hands away from her. Reasonable?"

He glared at me with those cold eyes, not dropping a word. He was the man a lot of the women in the camp admired. I had no doubt Helen was one of them. Despite the years, I still remembered how excited she was when I was bringing her into a meeting with him and some commanders from other camps.

I slid my hand from his shoulder to his chest. "She's my subordinate."

"So? I have absolutely no idea what you mean."

I swallowed, and I could feel a fire in my stomach. He didn't think I was here just to mock him, right? And if I was serious about busting him and putting him on the chopping board, we wouldn't be here alone. There would be other people here, judging. Although outside was dangerous and no form of government existed, other commanders would still pay close attention to what was happening here.

He might think I wanted him to apologize to Helen. Many admired him, and... maybe it was wrong for me to even think of that. But... He didn't get to touch my subordinate without my approval.

I said, "I would rather you let me know about you... urges and needs." My hand slid down to his stomach. Even over his military uniform, I could feel his abs.

Tempting. "I can entertain you instead of letting you bother my subordinates."

He smirked, and seemingly caught on. He lifted my cheek. "Be careful about what you're asking for."

"You are the one that should be careful. Why not solve things between us?"

His eyes darkened with lust and my hand slid to his crouch. My heart skipped a beat when I felt his throbbing hardness. He was larger than I expected. What was I getting myself into?

He took steps forward and forced me back to his desk. "Honestly, I've never seen you in this light." His gaze lingered on my breast as he let out a husky breath.

I rested my hand on his chest as he seemingly was eyeing me over. "I've never seen you in that light, either. Who would have guessed there's such a dangerous man here in the camp? And how can I forgive myself for sending my assistant into danger?"

"Danger?" He snatched my throat and tightened his grip until I was choking, but not bad enough I would die. He licked his lips. "You have no idea what danger means."

Before I could talk back, he shoved his hand between my legs. "Doc, I've never imagined you to be such a slut. You are coming here to ask for my cock fucking your pussy?"

I shivered. His very commanding growl made my body hot. Maybe I really needed someone to put me in my place. No one could do the job better than him. "Commander, do you need me to tell you what to do?"

He swore under his breath and put me on his desk. "It seems you really need to be taught a lesson."

"How are you going to do that?" Before my sentence even ended, he pinned my shoulder to the desk and hovered over me. I like how dominant he was and fuck that, those cold glares turned me on.

He reached into my robe, yanked off my panties, and rubbed my pussy. "It seems you've been wanting this."

His fingers were crazy on their own. The pulses of pleasure tore through me, making it hard to even form a word. But I just wasn't someone that would keep quiet. He also knew that about me, and he probably liked to hate me for that. We were the rival in the camp that everyone knew. He just needed some prompt and he would have no problem taking me like a beast.

He snickered as he watched me squirm. "Are you sure this is what you want? I think it is clear as day how much I hated you. As if you haven't provoked me enough in all the meetings and during the long years of us working together?"

If he would keep his fingers working on me, and later give me his cock, then whatever he wanted to say would be fine with me. "Doesn't those moment makes this even better? Time for you to take revenge? Trust me, I know how much you hate me."

Those cold gazes threatened to swallow me in a fire. Fuck that. He could make me come just by staring at me like that. I guess I really was that much a slut for punishment.

He squeezed my boob, and I squealed. He said, "That is a very pleasant thought. You have no idea how much I've been wanting this and you're now putting yourself into my hands."

"Or under your body? I guess this is the only chance you can get to put me under you."

He slapped my pussy and almost shoved me through the roof with pleasant pain. I moaned, and he seemed satisfied with it. "Doc, you're such a dirty slut. Had I known, I would have fucked you long ago."

"Before you put a hand on my assistant, I do have some respect for you. No — ! I'm sorry!"

He pulled back his fingers, and he obviously had the enjoyment of watching me squirm and almost had to beg for him to touch me. He said, "I would strongly suggest that you mind your words. Are you jealous of her?"

I bit the inside of my mouth. Despite the emptiness inside me, I could never seem to control my mouth when it came to him. The urge to come off on top was always there with me. "Now you're admitting it."

"No, I'm just asking a question that has nothing to do with that." There was a low thud of his belt falling onto the floor. "Tell me, are you jealous of her?"

If I wanted the good things, maybe I should give him the answer he wanted, but my ego wouldn't allow it. "It depends on what you have to offer. I'm not going to be jealous if you only have — "

Fuck, he was huge. He rubbed his tip on my entrance, sliding up to my clit and more, showing off how thick and how long he was.

"Doc, I really think you are smarter than that."

"Commander, I'm smart enough to know empty words from actual results."

He growled and pressed his monster-like cock inside me, stretching me to the maximum. "You're never going to make it easy for me, huh?"

I wrapped my arms around him as he pushed deeper and deeper inside me. He really was the commander everyone knew to fear. He was great in battles and apparently even better with his cock. "Commander, is this the first day you know me?"

"Know you as a slut that is so hungry for me? This, for sure, is the first day."

I moaned, and pussy clenched tight on him. "I have to make sure what had distracted my assistant, after all, right? Efficiency, the thing you've been emphasizing around here."

He snorted a laugh as he started moving inside me and fuck; it was hard to not come from that strong rub from him.

I took a deep breath. If he could make me come within minutes, that was a bit too embarrassing and a bit too ego-stroking for him.

He undid my robe and lifted my clothes, exposing my boobs. He pinched my nipples as he rammed inside me. "Apparently, you do pay quite some attention to me."

"Who don't... when... I hope you aren't also too efficient that you're going to come inside me this soon."

His cock twitched inside me. He was clearly ready to chew my head off. "Don't think of yourself too highly, doc."

He wrapped his fingers around my neck, stroking my throat with his thumb. "When you can't even walk from how hard I'll make you come. Don't cry."

"Trust me, I won't even have to risk that. And you better work harder, commander."

He bit on my boob. Hard enough to make me screamed, but not hard enough I bled. "You better mind that your mouth."

He picked up speed and hammered me harder and harder until the desk shook with his force. I wrapped my legs around him and arched. I could imagine he was good, but he was exceeding my imagination with every thrust.

I said, "You know me, that's never going to happen."

Fuck, he really knew what he was doing and…

"No!" I screamed when an orgasm hit me hard. I had tried to hold it back, but I failed. My juice spilled and my whole body tensed.

He laughed, and as I expected, he was enjoying how much of a mess I was and especially how he was the one making me a mess. "Doc, look at you. Are you sure you can keep talking like that and expect me to be kind to you?"

I smacked his chest, but it was obviously too weak to even shake him. "That's an accident." Another wave was coming up again. I didn't even know how he could work that in with his cock.

"Oh yeah? Then you should be glad you're mostly in the lab. Outside, enough accidents and you'll be pretty much dead." He hammered inside harder and pinned my shoulders back onto the desk again. He was so eager to make me come again.

"Commander! I..."

He was moving quicker and quicker. I couldn't even control myself anymore. How could I hate him that much while at the same time letting him slam in this kind of pleasure?

I screamed, and he took hold of my body and my mind. He'd shut me up without even having to fuck me in the mouth. "Doc, tell me again how you're going to keep talking back? You know it'll end up better for both of us if you'll just shut up."

"You..." It was so hard to even come up with words. The office room was filled with my moans and how our bodies ran into each other. He must have planned it. The dirty sound he made with my pussy was a bit too annoying. "You... 'd miss my moan if I'll actually shut up."

He snickered. "Trust me, you can't even not moan and scream my name."

"Kendrick!" I yelped at once. He didn't prefer the use of his first name. He was also of a rank no one dared to use that.

In this camp, there was only me that was his equal in terms of rank. And for sure, his equal when it came to arguing and with the power to command the team.

I usually still referred to him as the commander, just so it wouldn't be awkward for others and I didn't need to seemingly flex how I was in the same rank as him. But not now, for sure, especially not when he was asking for it.

His gaze darkened, and he pinched my nipples so hard I squealed. "Eve, you have to do that? Trust me, you love to get fucked a bit too much."

"Is that even a surprise? I'm the one here in your office."

"Eve, beg for my cock."

I was going to laugh at that when he pulled out of me with that evil smirk. I sat up at once. I was so close to another peak and he...

His erection was there, mocking me, still shiny with my juice. I swallowed just from staring at him. My cheek was burning. This wasn't the first second he had a full view of my naked body, but now it was obvious and his gaze on me was a bit too hot.

"Eve, you're a smart woman."

The emptiness inside me shouted for me to just ask and humble myself. But... I bit the inside of my mouth. How dare he use my body as a weapon to fight me? I shivered, chewing the pulsing desire inside me.

He had that smirk that was so confident I doubt this was something he came up with all of a sudden. He must have done the same to other women and resulted in them begging to be fucked. But that wasn't going to happen to me. Maybe he had that very tempting cock.

Still, no.

"Doc, did you hear me?" His glare turned cold. And fuck, that was quite something. If he kept doing that, he could make me come and that couldn't happen. It would be worse than if I beg for him.

"Commander, you know that's never going to happen." I reached my hand to my soaking wet pussy and rubbed myself. "If you're so scared that you would come before you can have the fun teasing me, I understand. I have no problem entertaining myself and you can leave with your poor cock."

"Fuck..." He growled and his cock twitched. I couldn't be the only one hating how he pulled out of me. I swore he also wanted to fuck me and he may want it even more than me. His husky breath filled the room as I played with myself.

If anything, I would pretend to come because of my hand instead of coming because he was staring at me like that.

"Commander, stop being so stubborn. Why fight me? We could be having fun together and you have to spoil that. You can't even blame me when you're the one pulling. Grow some balls."

He growled and before I could blink, his hand was on my throat, and his giant cock thrust inside me. Yes! He was the one backing off, not me. He squeezed on my throat, but apparently, it only made the pleasure stronger. "You are so annoying. Whatever and whenever it is about, you have to fight me in every detail."

I wrapped my legs around him, if he planned to pull out of me again, he won't succeed. "Commander, just admit it, you like how I keep fighting you."

"Your pussy is that hungry for me?"

"Such a change of topic, huh?" I smirked at his red face. I wasn't sure whether it was from how hard he was fucking me or it was from how I was turning him on.

His cock twitched and grew hotter inside me. He was getting close now. He picked up speed, giving me all the sweet pleasure. He hissed. "It seems you really need to be put back in your place."

My cunt contracted around him, and his cock pulsed, giving me his hot cum. He pressed to the deepest of me, sending me off into another orgasm. I panted and gasped to not drown from all the pleasure. He also closed his eyes briefly, seemingly also enjoying the moment.

I felt his chest; he was breathing heavily. "Commander..."

He opened his eyes and lifted his brows.

"I... Gosh, I sure have things to say that will piss you off."

He laughed. "I won't be surprised for sure. And when did you even care about that?"

"Hug me?" I didn't know why, but after letting him come inside me, I wanted some more closeness with him.

I was expecting him to refuse and at least tease me for another moment, but he didn't, and he wrapped me in his arms. "Doc, such a change, huh?" He lifted my chin and pecked a small kiss on the tip of my nose.

I asked, "I've been thinking that you hate me, am I right?"

"In terms of when we're in a meeting and you have to talk back to me, I hate you so much that I've wanted to fuck you for so long. Other times, no. I'm more professional than that. And side note, you also hate me."

"I... kind of. Like what you've said, when you have to keep coming back at me, I do hate you."

"But none of that is going to change even after you hand me your pussy, you know that, right?"

I snorted and leaned into him. "As if you can stop me with your cock. No, and if you keep being stupid, I'm going to call you out even more. I don't know how many times your poor body can take all those injuries."

"Ah, what's your worry?"

"The camp needs you."

"You can command the army if I'm dead."

I shivered. "You are a good comrade on that front. Don't die."

He kissed me with a softness I'd never seen in him. "Trust me, you'll need someone to put you in your place."

"With you and that cock? Think again." I hopped off the desk, but I stumbled. My legs were a bit too weak, and I hadn't expected it.

He held me before I would fall on my face. "I've told you I would fuck you so hard you can't even walk."

I regained balance and rolled my eyes. "Don't think of yourself too highly."

He snorted a laugh and leaned on the desk while I picked up my panties and tried my best to look decent. It was late now, but I still had a chance to run into someone.

As he fixed his belt, he said, "Now satisfied? Don't even mention that thing again."

What thing? How he laid hands on Helen? I would never give that an end. "What? Satisfied with what? Stop dreaming. You aren't as great as you've imagined yourself to be."

He glared at me and his gaze turned cold, just like the way I liked. "Right after you've screamed so hard and my cum is still hot inside you? Are you sure that's what you should say?"

I shrugged as I fix my hair. "What else am I supposed to say instead? You know I'll never make it easy for you and I'll have no end with you."

He hissed and leaned closer. I took a step back and rested my hand on his chest. He said, "Apparently, you still need to be taught."

"Commander, I'll look forward to that. You better make it good enough to not be a time-waster."

His lips crashed on mine like he was going to swallow me and fuck me over once again. I liked how his lips tasted and I like the fire and the lust inside him.

I said, "Remember not to put your hand on my assistant anymore."

He snickered. "Don't tell me what to do. I can only promise to put my cock inside you until you be a good girl for me."

I smacked his chest and rolled my eyes. I wasn't expecting to make him mine anyway. The pleasure itself was worth it. "Then you better keep waiting. At least you've healed up good enough."

Before he would grab me again, I left. It took an effort to pull myself from him. Was it wrong to blackmail him with what I knew between him and Helen?

As I walked back to my office and later back to my room for the night, his cum was still warm inside me and I wanted him again.

Maybe it was wrong, but then neither of us complained.

# Also By Mavis Lennon

Office Hour with My Boss

Singing for My Billionaire